To Finn,

it was all your idea!

First published 2018 by Two Hoots
This edition published 2019 by Two Hoots
an imprint of Pan Macmillan
The Smithson, 6 Briset Street, London, EC1M 5NR
Associated companies throughout the world
www.panmacmillan.com
ISBN: 978-1-5098-4270-4
Text and illustrations © Bethan Woollvin 2018, 2019
Moral rights asserted.

1 3 5 7 9 8 6 4 2
A CIP catalogue record for this book is available from the British Library.
Printed in China
The illustrations in this book were painted in gouache on cartridge paper.

www.twohootsbooks.com

Bethan Woollvin
Hansel & Gretel

TWO HOOTS

Deep in the forest lived a witch named Willow. Willow wasn't like most witches. She was a good witch, who only used good magic.

Willow had even made herself a home – entirely out of gingerbread.

One day while out in the forest, Willow spotted a trail of breadcrumbs which she decided to follow.

At the end of the trail, she found two children.

"We're Hansel and Gretel. What do you want?" demanded the children.

"I'm worried these breadcrumbs might lead birds and mice to my gingerbread home," said Willow. "Please could you help me clean them up?"

Hansel and Gretel didn't like this idea, so they left Willow to tidy up on her own. But Willow did not get angry, because Willow was a good witch.

When she arrived home, Willow couldn't believe her eyes.

"Hansel, Gretel, please don't eat my house!" Willow cried.

"But it's so tasty!" Gretel said, with a mouthful of gingerbread.

Hansel and Gretel must be very hungry, Willow thought to herself.
So she invited them in for dinner.

While Hansel and Gretel made themselves at home,
Willow used her best and most delicious spells
to cook up a feast for them all.

Unluckily for Willow, when she got to the table she found that Hansel and Gretel had already gobbled up all of the food!

But Willow did not get angry, because Willow was a good witch.

It wasn't long before Willow had more to worry about than her rumbling tummy.

Hansel and Gretel had found Willow's spells and wands, and began to play with them.

"Please be careful with my magic things!" Willow cried.

But Hansel and Gretel still would not listen.

The magic grew and grew and . . .

. . . grew!

Wanting the house all to themselves, Hansel and Gretel agreed to get rid of Willow.

Gretel pushed the witch into the oven and the naughty twins carried on filling her home with spells . . .

. . . until it was bursting
with magic!

It wasn't long before Willow's home collapsed. It was only made out of gingerbread after all.

But this time Willow did get angry.

Because Willow was not
ALWAYS a good witch.

FROM THE AUTHOR
Bethan Woollvin

I began writing *Hansel and Gretel* back in 2016.
I wanted to play with the reader's expectations and put a twist
on the traditional tale, so I wrote it from the witch's perspective.

But making books isn't always easy, and I struggled for some time with *Hansel and Gretel* –
I just couldn't find a satisfying ending to my tale. And so I looked to my younger siblings for
inspiration. After an afternoon of reading, drawing and making up hilarious
alternative fairytales, my little sister Freya accidentally finished my book.

Children truly have the best ideas. (Even if they can be a little wicked).

Thank you, Freya.

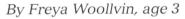

By Freya Woollvin, age 3